Mage T.M.

V-three

THE HERO DISCOVERED

BY MATT WAGNER

Mage

V-three

THE HERO DISCOVERED

Written and Illustrated
by Matt Wagner

Inked by
Sam Kieth

Lettered by
Bob Pinaha

Edited by Diana Schutz
and Rick Taylor

STARBLAZE GRAPHICS

THE DONNING COMPANY/PUBLISHERS
NORFOLK, VIRGINIA 1988

Mage—The Hero Discovered, Volume Three by Matt Wagner, is one of many graphic novels published by the Donning Company/ Publishers. For a complete listing of our titles, please write to the address below.

The Donning Company/Publishers
5659 Virginia Beach Boulevard
Norfolk, Virginia 23502

MAGE was originally published in comic-book format by Comico The Comic Company.

First printing October 1988

Library of Congress Cataloging-in-Publication Data

Wagner, Matt.
  Mage.
  1. Arthurian romances. II. Title.
PN6727.W25M3   1987   741.5'973   86-4487

ISBN 0-89865-465-3 (pbk: vol. 1)
ISBN 0-89865-560-9 (pbk: vol. 2)
ISBN 0-89865-616-8 (pbk: vol. 3)
ISBN 0-89865-615-X (ltd. ed.: vol. 3)

Printed in the United States of America

Words and pictures—essentially, the two key components to which the phenomenon of comic books can be reduced, each dependent upon the other, with the latter maintaining dominance in conveying good graphic storytelling. But it is the words . . . the words that inarguably help provide meaning and an explanation for the events that are graphically depicted, the words that help move *forward* the depicted events and, certainly, define and shape the characters to whom we endear ourselves or to whom we take an instant dislike.

In a sense, this is the manipulation that we, as readers, give ourselves up to for the sake of entertainment. And it is only successful when we allow ourselves to willingly be manipulated, then can walk away, still caring and thinking about the fictional characters and situations that we've just encountered. That's the success of a good story.

Welcome to the success of Matt Wagner and *Mage: The Hero Discovered.*

As letterer for the series, I have the proud distinction of being the only other person connected with the story throughout its complete fifteen-issue run. And, as I look back over these Donning editions, it doesn't seem so long ago that I was first approached to work on one of two color books Comico (the original publisher of *Mage*) was introducing to the field, in its attempt to become a strong force in the comic book marketplace.

Back then, I was sent one sample page from something called *Evangeline* to letter, along with another photocopy, this being the second art page to the first issue of *Mage.* You can imagine my puzzlement in looking over the script for this page, and, admittedly, my initial disappointment. There were *no* super-heroes to be found (something which I thought was *standard* in the medium), nor was any action to be found, as in the *Evangeline* sample page. However, I put my best effort into each sample, secretly hoping that I'd be chosen for *Evangeline.*

No such luck! *Mage* was the assignment I was given, an assignment that I determined to challenge myself with, in order to maintain some interest in what appeared to be a relatively passive series.

Soon after, I received a call from Matt detailing his plans for the fifteen-issue run, telling me a bit of what the series was about and how it would conclude, and letting me know when the first batch of pages would arrive for lettering. Yet, when they did arrive, well, truth to tell, I was scared to touch them! (A good thing, too, for, several days later, I received a phone call from Matt requesting a script change: he wanted the word "glaecken" that appeared throughout to change to "grackleflint." "Glaecken . . .? Grackleflint . . .?" thought I, too ashamed to admit that I had yet to look over the script. "Could I be in over my head here?")

As you can probably figure out, I overcame my fear of touching these somewhat mystifying art pages. But, more importantly, I found myself growing with the characters and developing along with them as well.

And, soon thereafter, certainly much sooner than even *I* anticipated, the initial disappointment gradually turned into intrigue, as I found myself getting caught up in the unfolding events that Matt was weaving and masterfully shaping with each passing page.

And you know what? You'll find that, after reading this third, and last, volume, you'll reach the same conclusion that I and many other fans have already reached . . .

Mage is a good story.

Enjoy!

—Bob Pinaha
June 1, 1988

Last Time . . .

As the Red-Caps attack, Mirth cautions Kevin of the power of their elf-bolts here on their home plane. Even so, Kevin soon makes short work of the three goblins and chases Lazlo to a narrow escape via elevator. Forceful but hesitant, Kevin jumps down the shaft and crashes directly through to the bottom. He is soon retrieved by Mirth, though, and they proceed to escort the shaken Sean from the Faerie Realms. Mirth then begins to explain that Sean must surely be dead.

All through this, the Umbra Sprite has sent his shade to appear before Rashem and Gregory. Claiming to be the Big Good Angel of Rashem's spirit and using voodoo vernacular, the shade seduces them with the gift of what appears to be a magic staple gun. Exiting the Faerie Realms, Mirth details what *he* says is the only answer to Sean's mysterious presence and his other various extra-normal attributes, Sean is a ghost who has forgotten his own death. Eventually this fact is proven and Sean concedes to aid in this obviously inescapable situation. The three companions exit the Faerie Realms via the rear entrance of the police station. They are unaware, though, that Rashem and Gregory have also been magically released and are tailing them on their way to Edsel's. Eventually, the hunters lose track of their prey, however, as they stop to experiment with their staple gun.

Edsel, who has been grounded by her father since the arrest, is more than ready to go, and so they set off, reunited, for Kevin's apartment. Upon arriving, Kevin heads for his bedroom to change his well-worn clothes. Waiting for him, however, is a Leanhaun Sidhe—a Faerie mistress who proceeds to seduce him. Luckily, Mirth happens to peek in on the scene and realizes what is happening. Edsel and bat soon come to the rescue but while the battle rages, Sean envisions Stanis Grackleflint aerially spying on them. Mirth promptly sets chase and soon bags his prey. Deciding to question the hostage, Mirth hangs Stan from the shower (Gracs can't stand water) and invites Sean alone to be in on the interrogation. Sean, as a ghost, can project fear and is needed to obtain information non-violently.

The session soon reveals that Mirth, himself, is the magic beacon that has been guiding their enemies to them again and again, and he announces to the company that because of this, he must leave them. During this respite, Stanis succeeds in summoning his father's shade to again come to his aid and, so, escapes. The breakout is soon discovered, though, and Kevin leaps from the front hall window as Stan tries to make off in a stolen VW. The attempt ends with disaster, as the car eventually crashes headlong into the front of Kevin's apartment building and erupts in a violent explosion. Mirth has barely managed to teleport the others to the safety of Edsel's car, and then forces the bereft and shaken Kevin to join them. Later, Mirth says his goodbyes and proceeds to lock himself away in an instant-teller computer. He grants Kevin a magic access card to contact him in emergencies, but then is gone. Over the next five months, the three remaining companions take to impersonating beggars and street-dwellers in an effort to encounter their enemies as they, in turn, search for the elusive Fisher King. On one particular encounter, a laundry ticket is found in the pants of a Red-Cap who had accompanied Lazlo and Radu Grackleflint. Kevin and Edsel head for Sean's apartment (their latest headquarters), unaware that they are being followed by the two invisible Gracs. Later, persuing the laundry lead, Sean discovers a link to the ornate Styx Hotel and Casino. It seems there are five almost identical pit bosses at the casino, which has lately been sponsoring quite a bit of mission work amongst the downtown street dwellers. In fact, there is a party that very evening to commemorate the grand opening of a new facility. At the Styx itself, the indulgent Umbra Sprite is lulled into a false sense of security over news of the enemy camp, brought to him by Lazlo and Radu—unaware of the fact that his rivals are at that moment preparing to enter his sanctum.

Once inside, our heroes decide to split up and agree to rendezvous at the entrance in an hour. Both Kevin and Sean are soon spotted by the disguised Gracs and they promptly alert their father to the drastic situation. The Umbra Sprite sends a will-o'-wisp to lure Kevin to a remote elevator where he is then mesmerized by a pair of Faerie musicians. He wakes to find himself pinioned by a hairy, disembodied arm to the ceiling of a bottomless pit.

As the Umbra Sprite proceeds to terrorize Kevin over the gaping hole, Edsel and Sean, worried over Kevin's failure to show, succeed in capturing Piet and force him into escorting them to his father's office. Sean, peering through the walls, tells Edsel of their friend's predicament. The headstrong bat-wielder promptly batters her way into the pit and a battle soon erupts. Kevin, heartened by Edsel's appearance, manages to tear himself free, and the three soon escape into the less ethereal hallways of the Styx.

As they round the last corner to freedom, Emil suddenly pops forth from a seemingly solid wall and skewers Kevin squarely in the chest with his spur.

THE HERO DISCOVERED

MAGE ™

CHAPTER 12

Defend me,
friends; I am
but hurt.

THEY HAVE ESCAPED.

YES, THAT IS OBVIOUS.

I NEVER EXPECTED YOU AND YOUR BROTHERS TO STOP THEM.

ONLY TO DELAY.

AND WHAT ABOUT YOU?

DAMN IT! WHY DIDN'T YOU DETECT THAT BAT?!

AGAIN, OBVIOUS. BECAUSE IT WAS HIDDEN.

HIDDEN?! BUT IT WAS AS GREEN AS--

EMIL! ENOUGH! THIS IS PRECISELY WHY I SENT YOU AND YOUR BROTHERS TO PURSUE THEM.

YOUR CONTINUAL ARGUMENTS WOULD'VE ONLY DELAYED ME FROM WHAT I HAD TO DO.

I HAVE DEALT WITH THE MATTER.

A-HACCGH! KOFF! KOFF! KOFF! KOFF! ...koff...koff...

AND HOW HAVE YOU DONE THAT? LOOK AT YOU! YOU CAN BARELY MOVE!

I HAVE SUMMONED HELP. THAT IS WHAT WEAKENS ME. I HAVE BEEN MADE VERY BUSY THIS EVENING. IT WILL TAKE LONG TO RECOVER.

WELL, YOU NEEDN'T HAVE BOTHERED. I MANAGED TO SPUR MATCHSTICK! HE IS POISONED.

WELL AND GOOD, EMIL KOFF! ... B-BUT YOU FORGET...

...THAT, OBVIOUSLY, THEY MUST KNOW WHERE MIRTH IS. SURELY HE WILL RETURN TO HEAL MATCHSTICK, WHICH IS GOOD NEWS FOR YOU, TOO. MAYBE HE WILL HELP YOU WITH YOUR ELBOW.

I KNOW I WILL NOT.

AND, SO, TO PREPARE FOR THE REUNION OF THIS PATHETIC LITTLE CIRCLE, I HAVE INVITED OVER A GUEST OF WHAT I FEEL IS, FINALLY, SUITABLE STATURE--

--THE WORM OF THE MISTS, CROMM CRUICH.

HIS ARRIVAL HAS COST ME DEARLY, BUT HIS VISIT WILL PROVE FINAL, FOR NONE OF THEM HAS THE POWER TO RESIST HIM.

PIET IS "DRESSING" HIM NOW.

AT LAST, I WILL BE RID OF THEM.

THIS IS IT.

THANKS.

HOW'S HE DOIN'?

STILL BREATHING.

THAT'S ALL.

DAMN.

GET HIM UP TO MY ROOM. WE'LL STICK HIM IN BED. I SUPPOSE WE SHOULD KEEP HIM WARM.

YEAH, I GUESS.

HAVE YOU NOTICED THERE'S NO BLOOD?

YEAH, I SAW IN THE CAB.

TAKE HIS OTHER SHOE OFF. I'VE GOT TO GET OUT OF THIS GET-UP.

I WONDER HOW THEY MANAGED TO CAPTURE HIM IN THE FIRST PLACE...?

PROBABLY MAGIC. KEVIN'S *STILL* NOT VERY KEEN ON THAT STUFF. *HOWEVER* THEY DID IT-- THEY GOT HIM.

AND THEY GOT HIM *BAD*.

NO SHIT.

WELL, HOW THE *HELL* DID *LAZLO* KNOW TO SHADOW ME LIKE THAT? THAT'S WHAT *I* WANT TO KNOW!

WHO KNOWS, SPOOK? LIKE YOU SAID, THERE'S A *LOT* OF THIS WE DON'T UNDERSTAND.

BUT...

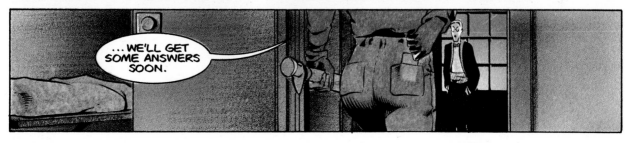

...WE'LL GET SOME ANSWERS SOON.

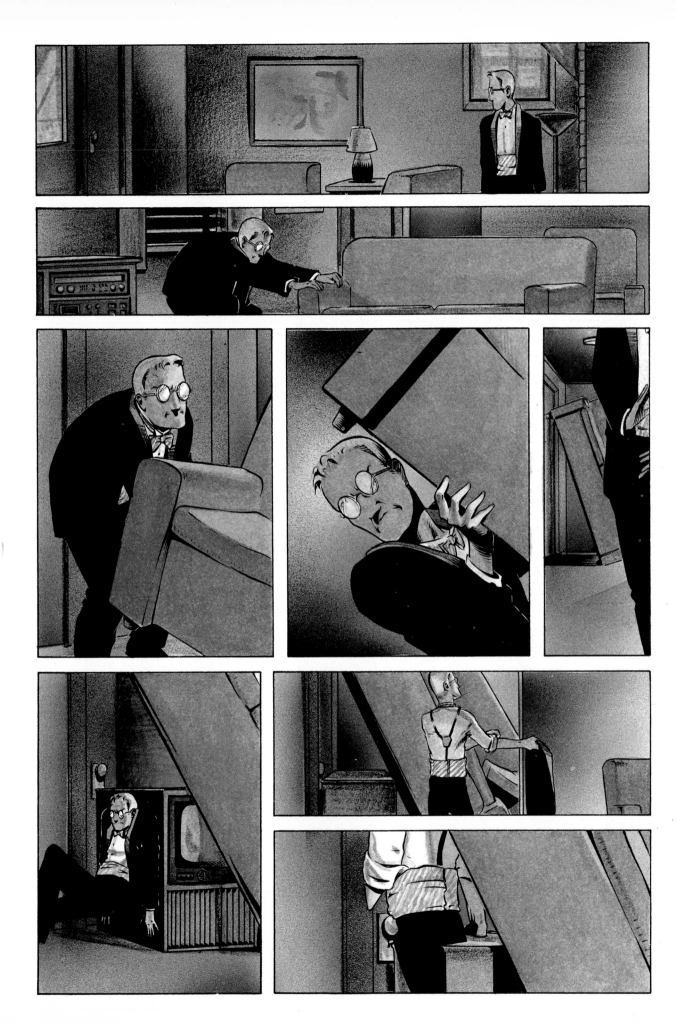

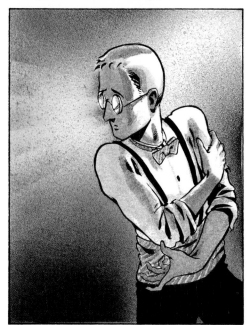

MORE OBSCENE.

FAR OLDER.

AND MUCH WISER.

MY RACE WAS DYING BEFORE YOURS LOST ITS TAILS.

WHILE YOU ARE SIMPLY A MAN WHO IS DEAD. YOUR AURA AND YOUR SUBSTANCE...

...THEY MEAN LITTLE TO ME.

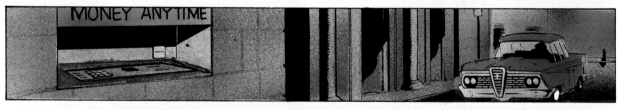

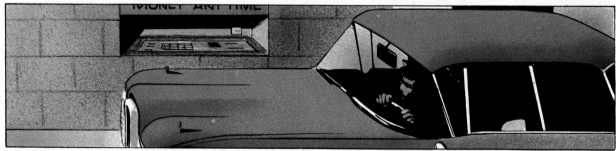

MAGE

NO. EDSEL. KEVIN SICK.

GRAC VENOM.

HELLO, MAGICIAN.

WHAT'S THIS?

SHOCK TRAUMA, I DO BELIEVE. IT'S BARREN IN *THERE*.

BUT--ENOUGH! QUICKLY! DESCRIBE KEVIN'S CONDITION TO ME.

WELL, HE WAS *STILL* BREATHING WHEN I LEFT, BUT SEEMED TO BE IN A COM--

ARRGHH!

MIRTH!

C-CROMM CRUICH.

WHAT?

I DON'T BELIEVE IT!

BELIEVE WHAT?

THE *UMBRA SPRITE*-- HE'S SUMMONED ONE OF THE *GREAT MIST WORMS!*

HUH?

IT'S SEAN...

...HE'S FIGHTING A DRAGON.

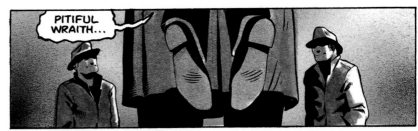

PITIFUL WRAITH...

...YOU ARE AS IGNORANT AS ALL YOUR VARIETY—A WANDERING SHADE WITH ONLY AN AXIOM OF POWER.

I SHALL SO ENJOY INCINERATING YOU.

AAGGHHGGG...

LET ME SHOW YOU.

TH-THAT WAS VERY UNCOMFORTABLE, SPIRIT.

EDSEL! WE MUST GO!

NO! SEAN! THAT--THAT BIG *FREAK*... HE... HE--

EDSEL!

LISTEN TO ME! SEAN HAS GONE. HE WAS *MEANT* FOR THIS. HE GAVE HIMSELF TO PROTECT KEVIN-- AS WOULD ANY OF US.

THAT "*FREAK*" IS THE DRAGON I SPOKE OF. WE CAN *NOT* FIGHT HIM.

SEAN HAS GAINED US TIME.

BUT NOW WE *MUST* LEAVE BEFORE HIS SACRIFICE BECOMES MEANINGLESS.

ALL RIGHT! THAT WAS WONDERF--

--UH... YEAH.

THE HERO DISCOVERED

MAGE ™

CHAPTER 13

Mark Me

CUZ THE
LOA DEE-SIRE
US.

SHUNT'A LEFT,
GREGORY...

JUS' SHUNT'A
LEFT.

TOLD YOU
THE GROS BON ANGE
WOULD COME
CALLIN' 'GAIN.

TOLD YA,
GREGORY.

AN'
WE SHALL
RE-JOICE!

I TOLD YOU,
GREGORY...

THE LOA'S
GONNA TAKE HOL'
OF OUR EYES.

YES, KEVIN?

WELL, I UNDERSTAND--*SOMEWHAT*--ABOUT THIS HOOKING UP *LAZLO* TO A RADIO SIGNAL IDEA...

...BUT HOW THEY GONNA DO IT?

WELL, SINCE WE'VE BEEN GONE, THIS STATION HAS BEEN PURCHASED, IN COMPLETE, BY THE *STYX* CASINO.

SO, OF COURSE, THEY HAVE COMFORTABLE ACCESS TO THEIR NEEDS IN THIS CASE.

AND IT MAKES OUR ENTRY TO THE PREMISES ALL THE MORE DIFFICULT, FOR THERE'RE *SURE* TO BE VARIOUS MAGICAL DEFENSES-- THUS, THE REASON FOR OUR REAR APPROACH.

HEY, WHY *THESE* DUDS?

OH, SOMETHING A BIT POETIC ABOUT IT-- START AS YOU BEGAN.

IF *THAT'S* SO, HOW ABOUT ALL THE HAIR I'VE LOST?

DON'T WORRY, KEV. YOU'RE *STILL* CUTE.

CUTE, HELL. I'M TALKING ABOUT ALL THE INNOCENCE I'LL NEVER KNOW AGAIN.

OH? WERE YOU SO VERY PURE AT THE BEGINNING, THEN?

AND IF YOU WERE, DID YOU *WANT* TO BE?

NOT SNOWY-WHITE, BUT *CERTAINLY* NOT AS MOTTLED AS *THIS*-- WITH DEATH IN MY HANDS...

...AND DEATH IN MY WAKE. DON'T TELL ME YOU PREFER THE PRESENCE OF DEATH, EDSEL.

NO, I *PREFER* THE ABSENCE OF FEAR.

AS DO WE ALL, BUT *I'M* AFRAID WE MUST BE MOVING ALONG.

THE DEFILER...

WE HAVEN'T MUCH TIME TO BEGIN WITH, AND I'M SURE *EMIL*, *PIET*, AND *LAZLO* ARE ALL INSIDE. SO, FOLLOW ME.

WHERE? TO MORE DEATH?

EVERY BREATH YOU TAKE BRINGS YOU CLOSER TO MORE DEATH, KEVIN--EVEN IF YOU STAND STILL.

I'M NOT EXACTLY SURE *HOW* THEY'RE PLANNING TO DO THIS, BUT I *AM* SURE THAT THEY MUST BE LOCATED SOMEWHERE VERY NEAR THE TOP.

MAYBE THE TWENTIETH FLOOR OR ABOVE--I CAN'T DIVINE THEM PRECISELY.

BUT WE ARE *BLOCKED* BY VARIOUS THINGS.

SUCH AS?

OH, CERTAIN PROTECTIVE WARDS. NOTHING *EXTREMELY* HARSH.

NOISY, THOUGH.

EXACTLY.

THE D-DEFILER...

...WHITER STILL...

IN FACT, WE HAVE TO OPERATE UNDER THE ASSUMPTION THAT THE *UMBRA SPRITE* HAS ALREADY DETECTED MY RETURN AND WILL SOON WARN THEM, ANYWAY.

THE LAYERS SEEM TO WEAKEN AS THEY GO UP, THOUGH.

SO, I'LL TRY TO DO THIS AS QUIETLY AS I CAN.

...M-MAUVAIS SANG...

...S-SPILL MAUVAIS SANG!

P-KOW!

AAAGHHH--

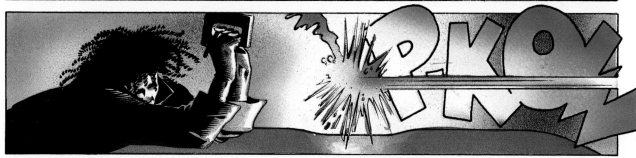

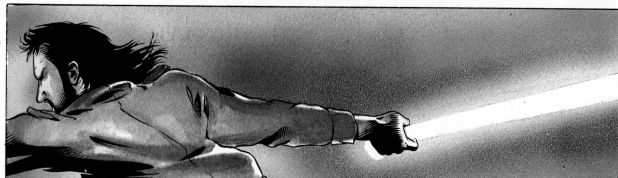

P-KOW! P-KOW! P-KOW! P-KOW!

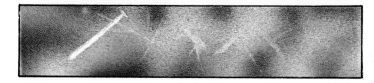

MAGICIAN!

NNHGHH-- D...DON'T LET THIS M-MESS YOU ALL UP. MIRTH'S RIGHT.

IT'S HAPPENED BEFORE. NOW I SEE WHAT HE MEANT WHEN HE SAID I WOULD BE THE CAUSE OF YOUR KNOWING.

UN-GGHHH!

EDSEL, PLEASE...

N-NO, KEVIN, SHUT UP. I HAVE TO TELL YOU SOMETHING. S-SOMETHING YOU WILL KNOW AS THE TRUTH...

AGNHHH--

...B-BECAUSE YOU'VE ALREADY TOUCHED IT.

COME HERE...

...MY LORD...

SHE WAS RIGHT.

YOU KNOW IT IS TRUE--

--BECAUSE YOU HAVE TOUCHED THE BAT, FELT ITS SERENITY AND ITS CONSUMPTION.

HER LINE HAS ALWAYS CARRIED THE WEAPON FOR YOU--

--AWAITING YOU AND THIS MOMENT.

YOU ARE THE PENDRAGON, WHO BEFORE WAS CALLED ARTHUR.

AND YOU CANNOT TURN BACK FROM WHAT HAS NOW BEEN AWAKENED--YOUR OTHER HALF...

THE HERO DISCOVERED

MAGE
™

CHAPTER 14

...Or
Not To Be

KEVIN?

I KNOW.

IT'S DELIRIOUS. BUT GO. TAKE IT.

IT'S YOURS.

YOU *CAN'T* WALK AWAY FROM THIS, KEVIN, AND YOU *CAN'T* TRANSFER YOUR GUILT ONTO ME.

THE GUILT YOU SEE IS YOUR OWN--YOUR FEAR OVER WHAT YOU *KNOW* TO BE THE TRUTH.

HAVE YOU NOT KNOWN *THIS* OF YOURSELF SINCE YOU WERE BORN? DOES *THAT* LIGHT SEEM SO VERY UNFAMILIAR?

FAMILIARITY ISN'T THE CASE. IT'S A MATTER OF DESIRE.

AND I *DON'T* WANT IT.

BUT WANTS AREN'T NECESSARILY THE WHOLE STORY, KEVIN. THERE'S A MATTER OF RESPONSIBILITY.

BUT *I* DECIDE WHAT I'M RESPONSIBLE FOR. THERE'S *ALSO* THE MATTER OF FREE WILL.

WELL, IN THAT CASE, SHOULDN'T YOU MAKE THAT *"PEOPLE ARE DYING ALL AROUND US"?*

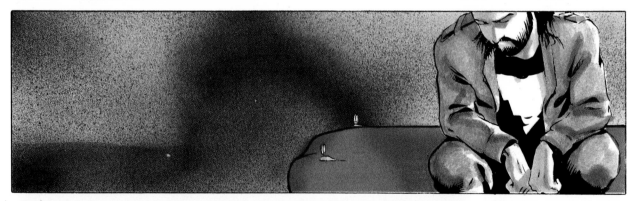

LOOK, MIRTH, I'VE *HAD* A PART IN ALL THIS, BUT ONLY AT YOUR INSISTENCE. AND LOOK AT WHERE *THAT'S* LED ME.

I HAVE NEVER *LED* YOU, KEVIN-- ONLY ADVISED.

WELL, THEN, WHO *WAS* THE LEADER? SEAN WAS AN ORGANIZER, BUT STILL AFTER YOUR LEAD.

AND EDSEL CERTAINLY DIDN'T LEAD HERSELF TO THAT.

IT'S A CHOICE THAT WE ALL HAD, KEVIN-- TO FOLLOW THIS PARTICULAR COURSE OR NOT.

ONCE COMMITTED, THOUGH, CONCLUSIONS ARE *INEVITABLY* MADE.

OR DO YOU THINK I *LIKE* HAVING MY LEG SHOT OFF?

I DON'T KNOW *WHAT* THE HELL TO THINK YOU LIKE, MIRTH. IN *ONE* RESPECT YOU'RE *BUBBLING* WITH EXCITEMENT...

...AND YET THERE LIES EDSEL.

SPARE ME THIS, KEVIN. YOU'RE ONLY SEEING IT FOR THE *FIRST* TIME.

MY AWARENESS OF THE SITUATION IS ALSO PAINFUL. YET I AM ECSTATIC TO SEE THE LOSSES NOT BE IN VAIN.

FOR, IF YOU'LL TRULY LOOK AT WHAT HAS COME TO BE, YOU'LL FIND WE DID IT ALL FOR YOU.

WE'VE FOUGHT FOR YOU. WE'VE SCHEMED FOR YOU. WE'VE *BLED* FOR YOU.

YOU'LL RECALL SEAN *CAME* TO YOU AS A DEFENDER. IN THE END, THIS HONOR *DESTROYED* HIM.

AND, OF COURSE, THERE IS NO QUESTION OF EDSEL'S DEVOTION. THE FIRE OF EXCALIBUR HAS BEEN CARRIED IN THE BREAST OF THE WOMEN OF HER LINE SINCE BEFORE EVEN *MY* VERY FIRST BIRTH.

BUT IT WAS SHE WHO WAS TO BE THE LAST. AND SHE CHOSE TO FOLLOW HER COURSE WITH A BRAVE HEART.

ALL BECAUSE HER VITALITY REMEMBERED YOU.

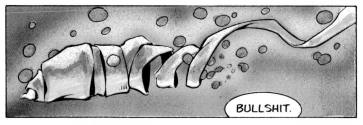

BULLSHIT.

THERE WAS NOTHING TO REMEMBER.

I SPEAK OF A MEMORY FAR DEEPER THAN THE SURFACE GLOSS YOU CONTINUALLY SWIM IN, KEVIN.

SHE KNEW HER CHANCES, YET SHE DID IT FOR YOU.

YOU ARE THE LEADER, MY FRIEND.

YEAH.

RIGHT.

I'M KING ARTHUR.

WELL, NOT KING, EXACTLY. AND NOT ARTHUR, EXACTLY. YOUR HEART IS THE HEART OF THE PENDRAGON RETURNED--CONFUSED AS IT MAY BE.

EDSEL'S ROOTS, TOO, ARE ANCIENT AND FEY. SHE USED TO LIKE LAKES INSTEAD OF CARS, BUT SHE HAS ALWAYS HELD THE WEAPON FOR YOU.

AND WHAT ABOUT SEAN? YOU'VE GOT TO ADMIT THAT HE WAS FOLLOWING THIS ALL THROUGH FOR HIMSELF-- TO PUT AN END TO HIS CONFINEMENT. HIS SACRIFICE WASN'T EXACTLY "FOR ME."

WELL, THEN, JUST WHOM EXACTLY WAS IT FOR? SEAN'S CONFUSION STEMMED FROM HIS SHOCK OVER THE BREAK IN HIS CALM ROUTINE. BUT, AFTER ALL, HE HAD DIED LATE IN THE FIFTIES--GAS LEAK, YOU SEE. HE REALLY WAS USED TO IT ALL. HE JUST DIDN'T KNOW IT.

ONCE OVER HIS INITIAL DOUBTS, THOUGH, HIS GOAL WAS STEADFAST.

NO, KEVIN, IF SEAN KNIGHT SERVED ANYONE, IT WAS YOU.

BUT I DIDN'T SEEK OUT HIS SERVICE--OR EDSEL'S EITHER. FOR THAT MATTER, I RAN INTO YOU BY CHANCE, TOO.

WELL, NO, I'M AFRAID THAT'S NOT QUITE SO, EITHER. I SOUGHT YOU OUT.

BUT WHY? WE'D NEVER MET BEFORE THAT NIGHT.

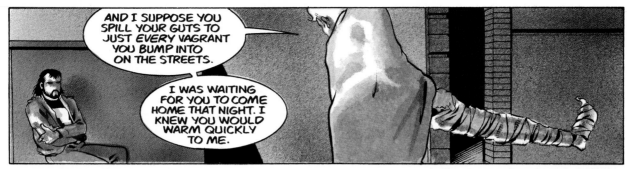

AND I SUPPOSE YOU SPILL YOUR GUTS TO JUST EVERY VAGRANT YOU BUMP INTO ON THE STREETS.

I WAS WAITING FOR YOU TO COME HOME THAT NIGHT. I KNEW YOU WOULD WARM QUICKLY TO ME.

COME NOW, KEVIN. REACH DEEP.

CAN YOU TRULY SAY THAT YOU HAVEN'T KNOWN ME FOR A LONG, LONG TIME?

YEAH.

OKAY.

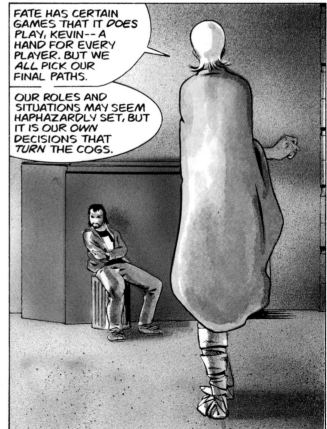

FATE HAS CERTAIN GAMES THAT IT DOES PLAY, KEVIN-- A HAND FOR EVERY PLAYER. BUT WE ALL PICK OUR FINAL PATHS.

OUR ROLES AND SITUATIONS MAY SEEM HAPHAZARDLY SET, BUT IT IS OUR OWN DECISIONS THAT TURN THE COGS.

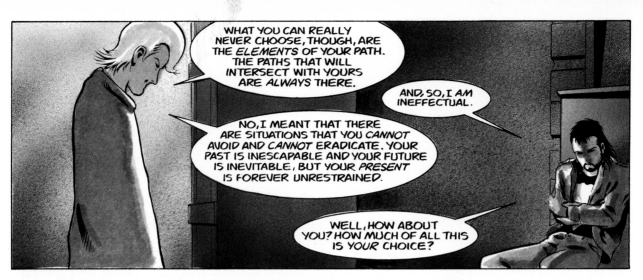

WHAT YOU CAN REALLY NEVER CHOOSE, THOUGH, ARE THE *ELEMENTS* OF YOUR PATH. THE PATHS THAT WILL INTERSECT WITH YOURS ARE ALWAYS THERE.

AND, SO, I AM INEFFECTUAL.

NO, I MEANT THAT THERE ARE SITUATIONS THAT YOU *CANNOT* AVOID AND *CANNOT* ERADICATE. YOUR PAST IS INESCAPABLE AND YOUR FUTURE IS INEVITABLE, BUT YOUR *PRESENT* IS FOREVER UNRESTRAINED.

WELL, HOW ABOUT YOU? HOW MUCH OF ALL THIS IS *YOUR* CHOICE?

I'M AFRAID *MY* ROLE IS SOMEWHAT MORE GOVERNED. FOR AGES AND AGES I HAVE BEEN A SERVANT TO THE STRUGGLE.

I SUPPOSE YOU COULD SAY I WAS THE STRUGGLE'S FOOL, AS I AM EAR TO ITS SECRETS BUT BONDED TO ITS DESIRES.

I SERVE THE WEAPON AND ITS WIELDER.

AND SO, YOU SEE, KEVIN, WE HAVE ALWAYS BEEN STUDENT AND TEACHER.

KING AND WIZARD.

HERO AND MAGE.

WELL, WHAT DO YOU DECIDE?

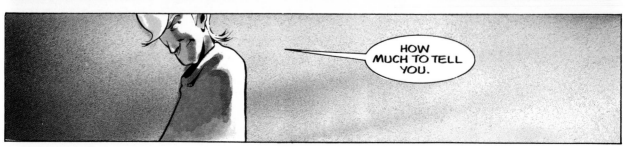

HOW MUCH TO TELL YOU.

THERE YOU GO AGAIN. YOU ADMIT THAT YOU'RE CONTINUALLY LEADING ME.

YOU TELL ME WHAT YOU THINK I SHOULD OR SHOULDN'T HEAR.

I TELL YOU WHAT I THINK YOU ARE READY TO HEAR. I'M AFRAID THAT'S THE WAY IT HAD TO BE.

OH, THANK YOU TOO MUCH.

YOU COULD NOT HAVE HANDLED IT ALL FROM THE START. IT WAS A NECESSITY.

BULL. I STILL CALL IT LEADING.

WOULD YOU HAVE PREFERRED TO ENCOUNTER THIS ALL BY YOURSELF? I TELL YOU I AM MERELY YOUR GUIDE!

OKAY, THAT'S WHAT YOU CALL IT. WHAT DO YOU CALL THAT?

I CALL THAT A GREAT SADNESS.

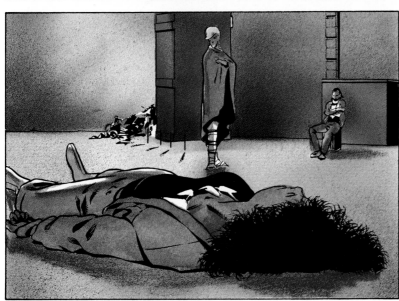

NO, KEVIN, THERE SHALL BE NO MINCING OF WORDS HERE.

I DO CALL THIS A GREAT SADNESS.

BUT THOSE WHO BEAR FOR YOU MUST OFTEN BE SHARPLY SWEPT AWAY...

...BEFORE YOU WILL BEAR FOR YOURSELF.

EDSEL

DAMN IT, KEVIN! SHE *BLED* FOR YOU!

AND, NOW, YOU REFUSE TO EVEN *FACE* HER FINAL MOMENTS!

HAVEN'T YOU GOT THE VALOR TO EVEN *LOOK* AT THIS?

OR DO YOU THINK THAT *THIS* WILL GO AWAY IF YOU REFUSE IT LONG ENOUGH, TOO?

DO YOU REALLY THINK YOU CAN FORGET HER?

LOOK, MIRTH, I DON'T TRY TO ERADICATE MY REALITIES. I TRY TO WALK BESIDE THEM IN TIME WITH KEEPING SANE.

AND, DAMN IT, SINCE I MET YOU I'VE BEEN RUNNIN' TRIPLE-TIME!

AND IS THAT *MY* FAULT, THE FAULT OF THOSE WE OPPOSE...

...OR *YOUR* OWN?

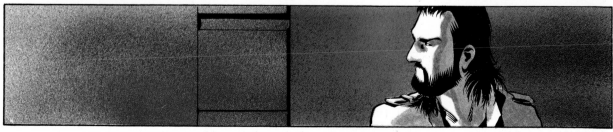

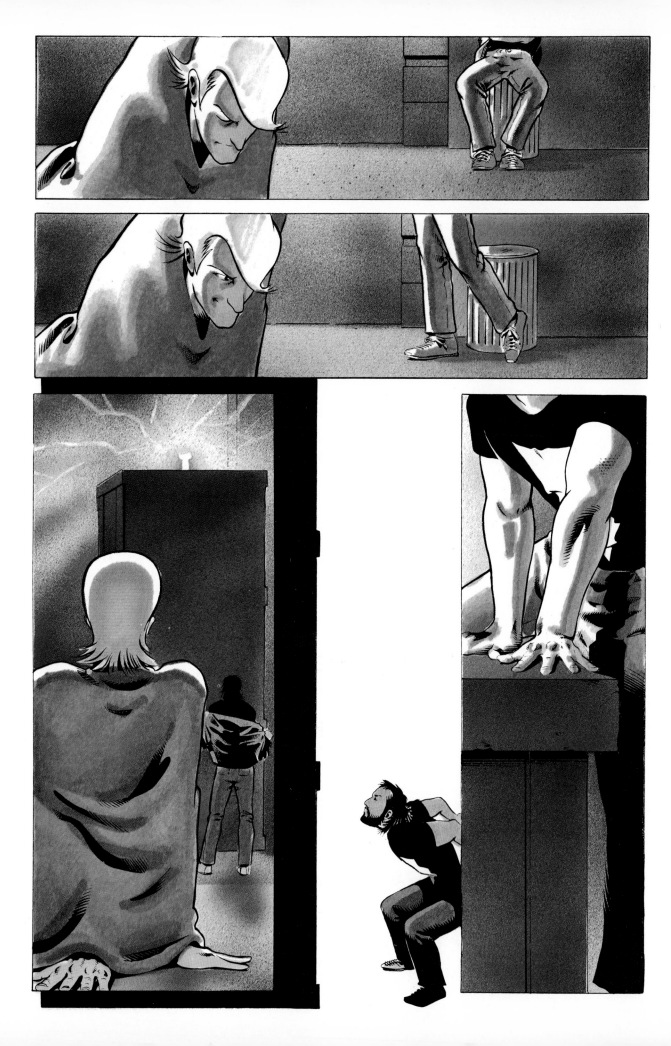

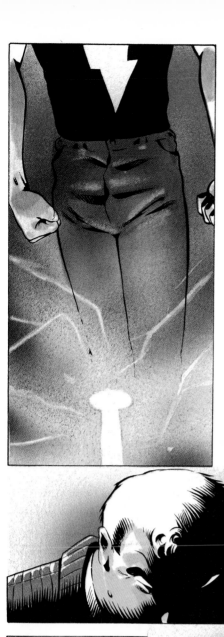

THE HERO DISCOVERED

MAGE ™

CHAPTER 15

Pass With
Your Best
Violence

COME.

WHERE?

HERE.

I "SAW" THEM LEAVING THE ELEVATOR AND HEADED TOWARDS THIS SIDE OF THE BUILDING.

THEY PROBABLY HAVEN'T EVEN LEFT YET.

QUESTIONS, FIRST.

WAIT.

WHAT?

I STILL DON'T UNDERSTAND THIS STUFF ABOUT LAZLO.

IF HE'S A VEG...

...HOW'S HE KNOW WHAT HE'S LOOKING FOR?

HIS FATHER'S PLACED HIM UNDER A POWERFUL SPELL THAT WOULD CAUSE HIM TO REACT UPON THE DETECTION.

MAKES HIM PRETTY USELESS OTHERWISE-- SO THERE'RE ONLY TWO.

HYPNOSIS.

YOU'RE SURE EMIL'S WITH THEM, THEN?

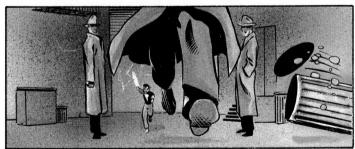

NOW, WHAT THE HELL'S ALL THIS?

WHO'RE THOSE GUYS?

THE ONE I TRIPPED...

...MUST BE PIET.

SHAPE-CHANGER.

YES. SENT AHEAD AS A DECOY.

THOSE TWO MUST'VE BEEN SECURITY GUARDS.

OH, GREAT.

JUST GREAT.

DAMMIT! I THOUGHT YOU SAID YOU WERE SURE!

THOSE WERE INNOCENT BYSTANDERS.

HIS ILLUSIONS ARE STRONG, KEVIN.

THE SIGHT ONLY SHOWS ME THINGS.

SOMETIMES THERE ARE PROBLEMS WITH THE TRANSLATION.

YEAH, SWELL. THAT MAKES ME FEEL REAL GOOD.

DAMMIT! I WAS READY TO ATTACK THOSE GUYS. I MEAN, THEY WOULDN'T HAVE KNOWN WHAT HIT THEM!

I WAS GOING TO HIT THEM...

...WITH THE BAT.

DAMMIT.

GO AHEAD, THEN...

...LAY IT DOWN.

YOU KNOW I CAN'T.

IT'S TOO SWEET.

I KNOW.

I'M SORRY. I SHOULDN'T HAVE BEEN SO CONFIDENT BEFORE.

I'M NOT INFALLIBLE.

BUT THE UMBRA SPRITE IS ALSO SO FLAWED.

IF ANY OF US HAD TOTAL VISION, NONE OF THIS WOULD BE NECESSARY.

WE WOULD SEE THE FISHER KING. BUT WE'VE LOST OUR OWN INNOCENCE...

...AND, SOMETIMES, THE INNOCENCE OF OTHERS.

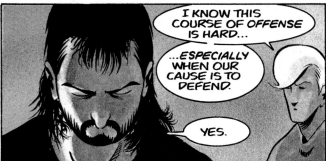

I KNOW THIS COURSE OF OFFENSE IS HARD...

...ESPECIALLY WHEN OUR CAUSE IS TO DEFEND.

YES.

HEY! OUR PRISONER'S RUN OFF.

LEAVE HIM.

WE DON'T NEED PRISONERS.

SO, YOU SEE, WE ARE LEFT WITH BUT ONE CHOICE.

TO TAKE THE FIGHT TO THE OPPRESSORS-- TO RETURN TO THE STYX.

JOY.

WELL? C'MON, THEN.

MIRTH?

WHERE ARE WE?

MIRTH?

WHERE THE *HELL* ARE WE?!

COME SEE.

OH, SHIT.

SORRY, KEVIN. SHOULD'VE WARNED YOU FIRST, I GUESS. DIDN'T THINK IT WAS NECESSARY, WHAT WITH THE BAT AND ALL.

WHAT D'YOU MEAN, "WITH THE BAT"? I CAN'T FLY WITH THIS DAMN THING, CAN I?

NO, BUT YOU'VE NOW MET UP WITH THE SOURCE OF YOUR POWER. A DROP LIKE THIS WOULD ONLY HURT THE SIDEWALK.

BESIDES, I THOUGHT YOU WERE OVERCOMING THAT FEAR.

NOT *THAT* WELL.

OH, GOD... AND ON THE OUTSIDE, YET.

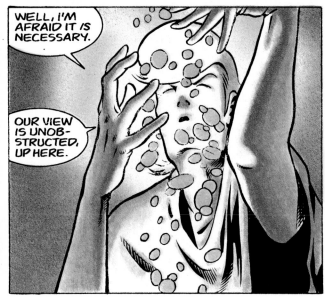

WELL, I'M AFRAID IT *IS* NECESSARY.

OUR VIEW IS UNOB-STRUCTED, UP HERE.

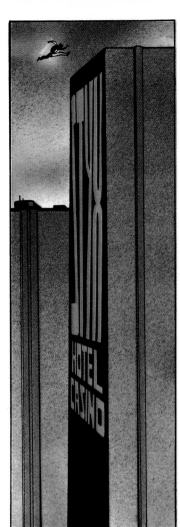
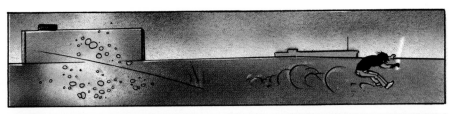

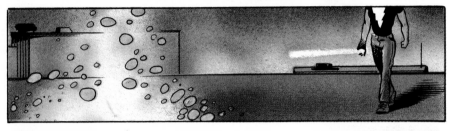

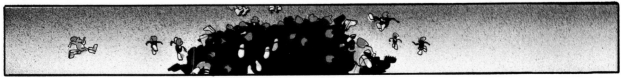

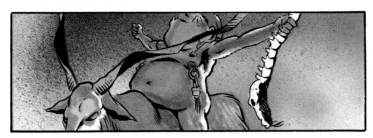

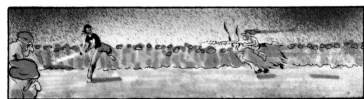

CLANG CLANG

CLANG CLANG CLANG
CLANG
CLANG CLANG CLANG

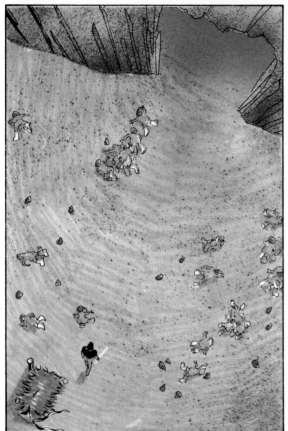

SNAP!

DAMMIT. NO TELLING *HOW* LONG THIS'LL TAKE. THE STREETS ARE FAIRLY FULL.

WONDER WHAT THE HELL HAPPENED TO PIET.

I'M NOT SURPRISED HE SCREWED IT UP, THOUGH. HE ONLY *EVER* HAD ABOUT AS MANY SMARTS AS *YOU* HAVE NOW.

WONDER WHY FATHER HASN'T TRIED TO CONTACT ME AGAIN.

SCREW HIM.

FAT TURD.

HE'S BLINDLY OBSESSED. HE ALWAYS *HAS* BEEN.

AND HE'S TAKEN US, THE *STYX,* AND EVERYTHING DOWN THE TUBES WITH HIM. SHIT-- HAVE YOU *SEEN* THE STYX'S PROFIT REPORTS THIS QUARTER?

NO, OF COURSE YOU HAVEN'T. WELL, BELIEVE ME, THEY STINK.

SCRAM, PUSS.

ANYWAY, THE *FISHER KING* APPEARS TO BE OUT OF THE QUESTION.

UNHHH--

B-BUT WHAT ABOUT FATHER?

SHIT! WILL HE EVEN CARE?!

OR IS HE TOO SODDEN IN HIS LITTLE BATTLE SCENARIOS? IS HE REALLY JUST A CASUALTY?

WHAT IS IT?

IT LOOKS LIKE THE STAIRS ARE OUT JUST AHEAD. I'LL CHECK IT OUT. WAIT HERE.

I DON'T NEED THE LIGHT.

KEVIN?

LOOK HERE.

SO BE IT. THESE DECISIONS WERE SET IN MOTION LONG AGO.

HE HAS CHOSEN HIS PATH--AND THE PATH OF THE OTHERS.

BUT MY VISION IS CLEAR-- UNTAINTED.

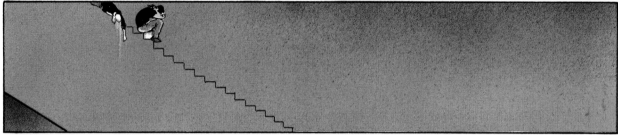

BITCH!

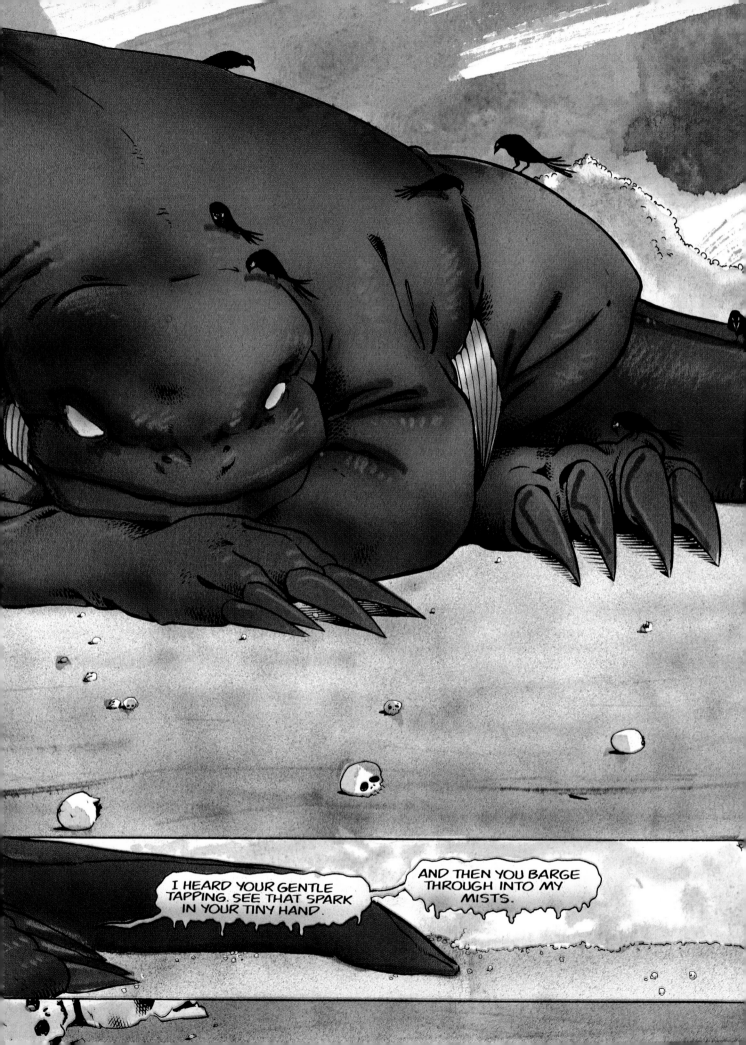

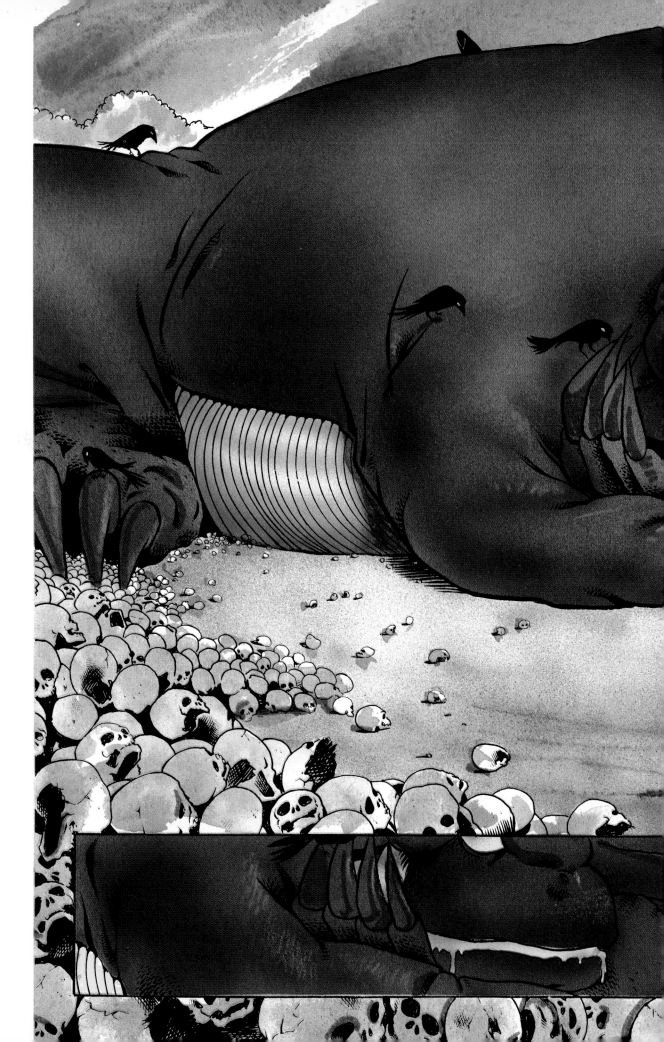

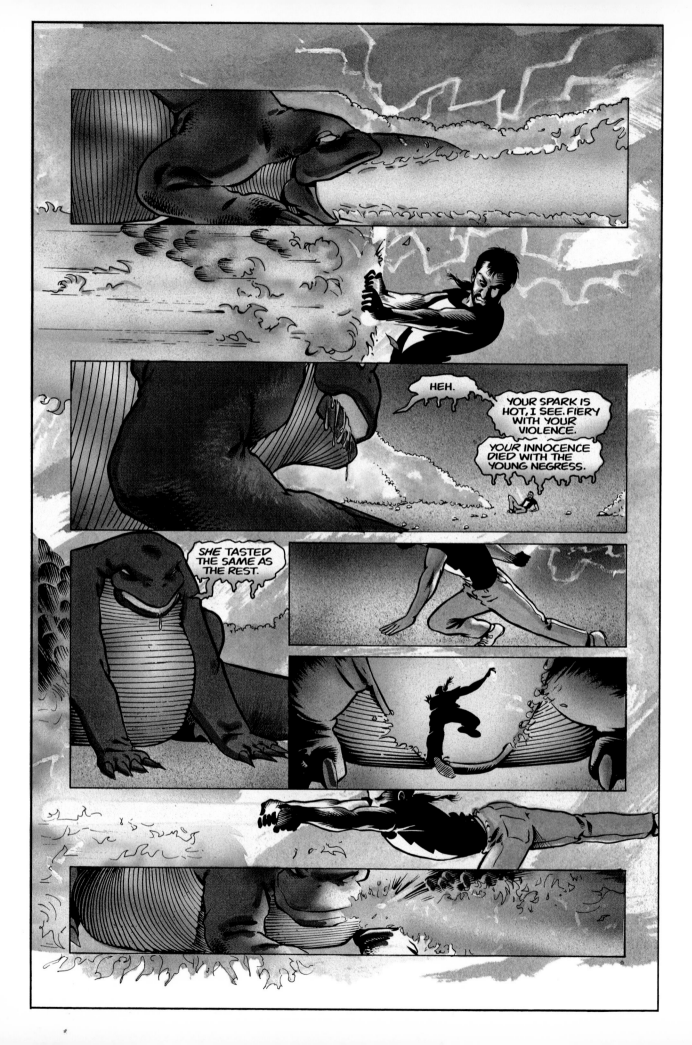

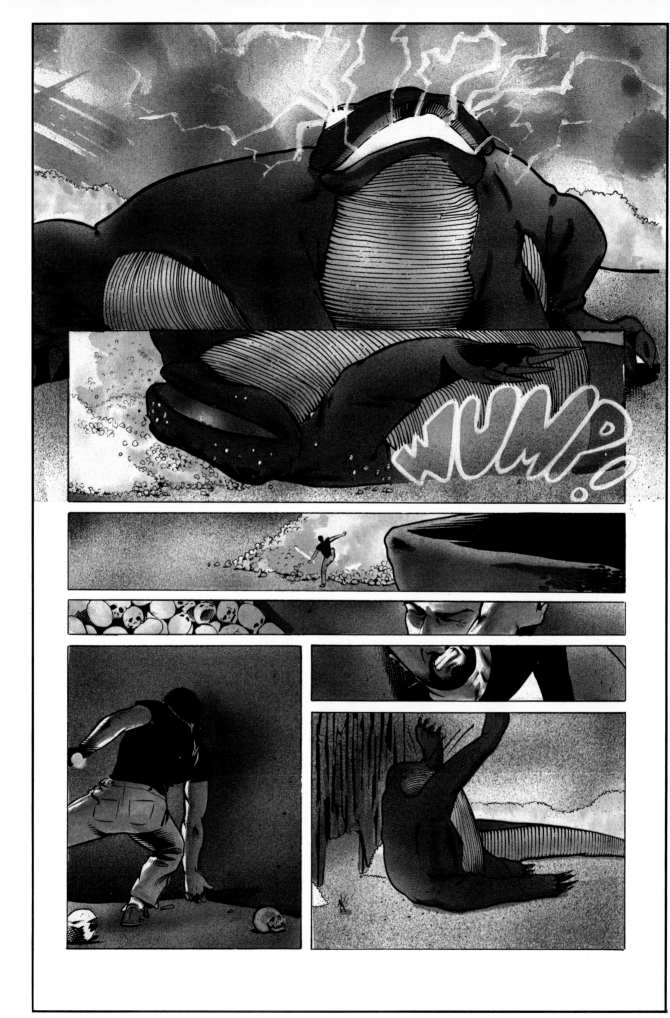

WELL?

AND WHO THE HELL ARE YOU?

HUH--?

OH.

SORRY. HUMPH-MPH... DIDN'T... HUMPH... DIDN'T SEE YOU. HMPH.

HMPH. NOT SURPRISED. HMPH-MPH. DAMN, YOU'RE TINY. HUMPH... GUESS DRAGON MISSED YUH. HUMPH.

JUST'S WELL. HUMPH. LONG TIME SINCE A TOSS-'N'-TUMBLE... HUMPH. EVER SINCE DRAGON MOVED IN. HMPH.

NAME'S GOE-MAGOT. WELL? SPEAK UP! HUMPH.

CAN YOU SPEAK? HUMPH?

SURE. KEVIN.

HUMPH. LITTLE NAME, TOO. HMPH. WE TUMBLE NOW. READY?

TUMBLE? WRESTLE?

YES, TUMBLE! HUMPH. YOU MUST. TO GO ANY FURTHER. HUMPH.

DIDN'T KNOW? HUMPH?

NO.

BESIDES...

...I CAN SEE THE EDGE OF THE PIT, THERE. WHAT IF I REFUSE AND JUST TRY TO CLIMB?

HUMPH... PUSH YOU OFF. HUMPH.

COME. TUMBLE NOW.

AND LAY ASIDE WEAPON.

LAY ASIDE...

HUMPH. SCARED, TOO?

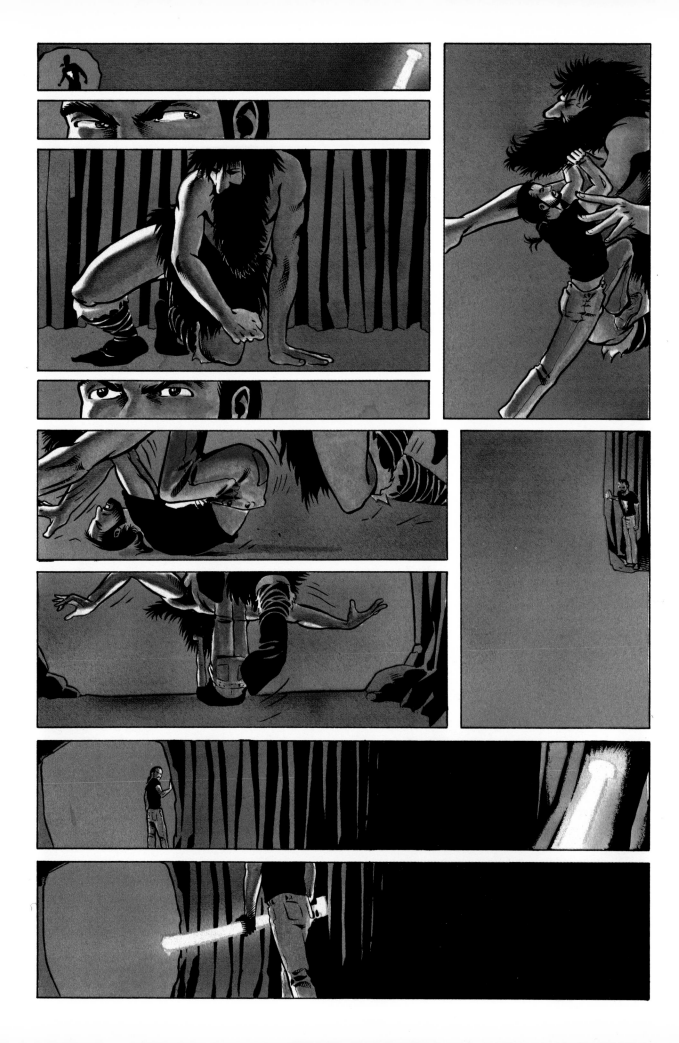

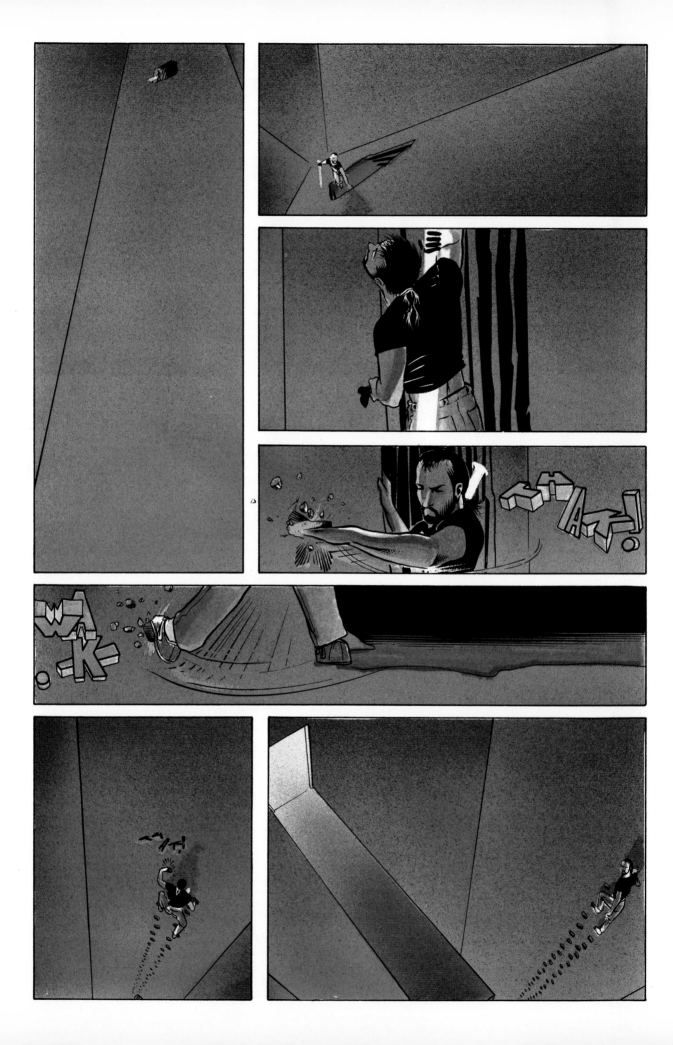

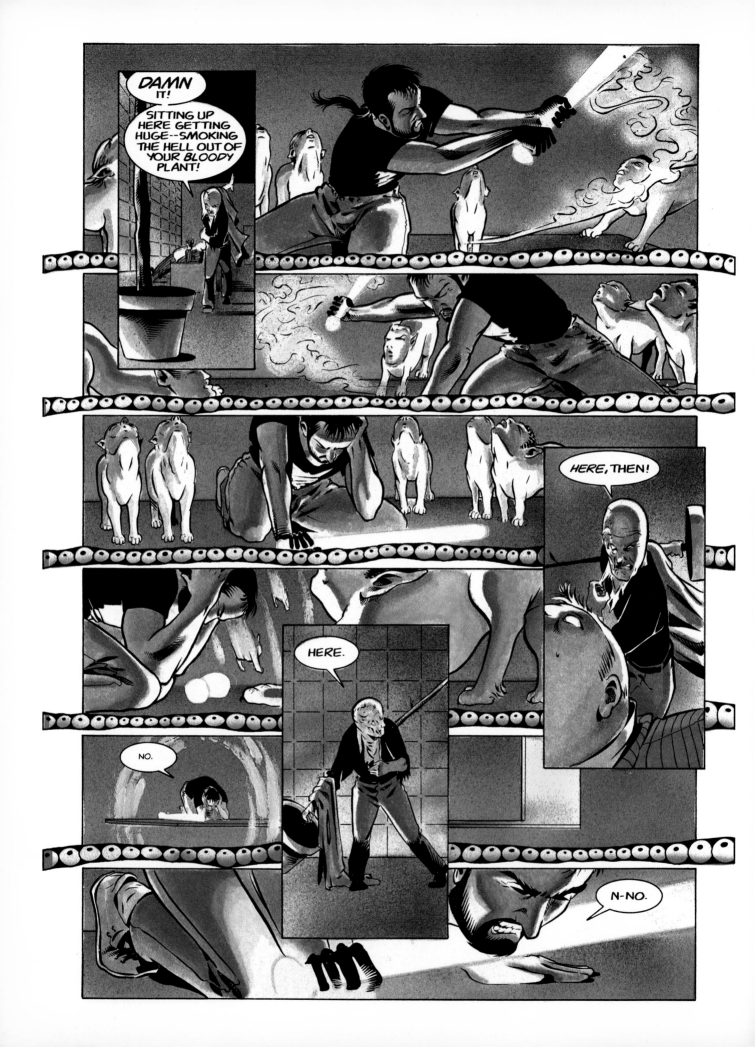

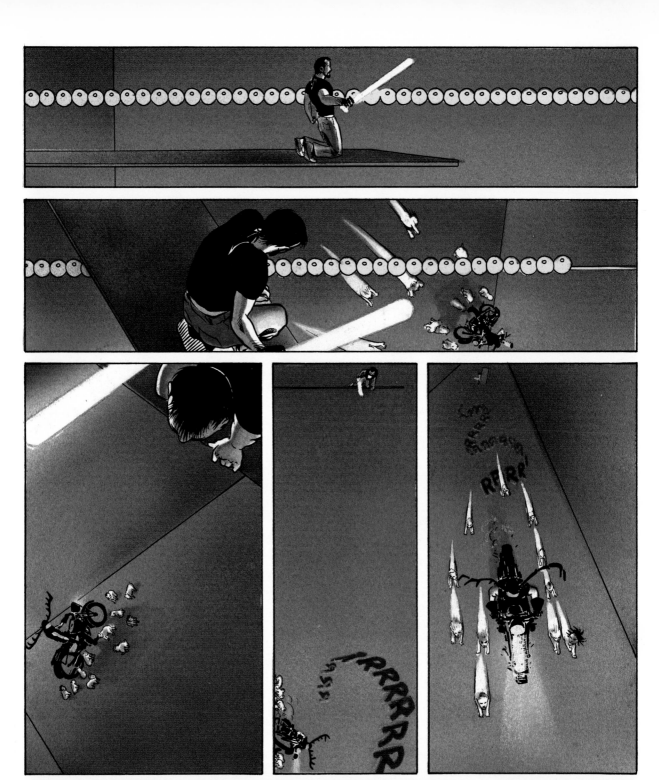

DIDN'T KNOW YOU COULD DRIVE.

LOTS OF THINGS YOU DON'T KNOW YET.

I SAIL, TOO.

ANYWAY, I HELD OPEN 'TIL I WAS SURE THINGS WERE LETTING GO, AND THEN STARTED SEARCHING AROUND FOR YOU.

YEAH, STARTED HAPPENING REAL FAST. TOOK A CHANCE. QUICK WAY DOWN.

HE'S DEAD, THEN?

YEAH, HE WAS LIKE THAT WHEN I FOUND HIM. BACK OF HIS HEAD CAVED IN. INSURRECTION, I GUESS.

HE WAS A LOT BIGGER, TOO.

WELL...

NASTY FRIENDS.

NASTY HABITS.

I WILL SAY YOU HARDLY PREPARED ME ENOUGH FOR WHAT I WAS UP AGAINST.

CHRIST, YOU WOULDN'T BE-LIEVE SOME OF THE STUFF I SAW IN THERE.

NO, YOU WOULD BELIEVE IT.

LEAST I DIDN'T HAVE TO DO IT ALONE.

NO. NEVER ALONE.

GOOD.

YOU SEE.

AND...YOU REALIZE, OF COURSE, THAT THE COLLAPSE OF THE STYX PROBABLY DIDN'T OBLITERATE THE DARKNESS.

MORE LIKELY JUST DISPERSED IT.

PROBABLY NOT, HUH?

NO.

YOU ARE NEVER ALONE, KEVIN, BUT YOU CAN NEVER TURN BACK-- FROM YOURSELF.

SO, WHO WANTS TO? HOW WE LEAVIN'?

GET IN.

Inquirer

Thirty-Five
Call 665-1234 for lower h

20

STYX FALLS

Chaos erupted last night as the Styx Hotel and Casino collapsed in on itself. Authorities are still sorting through the rubble and, as yet, can see no cause for the disaster. Luckily, the body count is low, owing to the Styx's closure of the last several weeks.

Having made recent heavy investments into FM radio WLYX, the Styx had been forced to effect a several-week peri-od of "inventory and reassessment." Thus, only a minimum of maintenance employees were present when the collapse occurred. As yet, no official announcements have been forthcoming from the owners of the Styx. Authorities claim they have yet to be located.

Cleanup, of course, continues in the Center City area.

(Cont. on pg. 3)

MASS HYSTERIA DUE TO CALAMITY

Following the collapse of the Styx last evening, authorities received an "amazing" number of calls reporting the ensuing chaos: everything from traffic accidents to group hallucinations. Peculiar, in fact, is the number of the latter. Police claim a wide range of fantastic voiced as to whether some element within the dust that was scattered over Center City was a factor in these common visions. Frequency and location of the reports would seem to support this, as these nightmares seem to spread outward from the remains of the Styx.

I'M DRIVIN'.

int

written & illustrated by

MATT WAGNER

letters by

BOB PINAHA

erlude

ÉTIENNE?

ΞSIGHΞ

ÉTIENNE?

HMPH...

MARIE?

ICI.

PAR ICI.

EN RETARD.

COMME D'HABITUDE.

MAMAN VA...

MAMAN.

MAMAN.

MAMAN.

JE M'EN FOUS DE MAMAN.

APRÈS TOUT...

...TU M'AIMES, N'EST-CE PAS?

PEUT-ÊTRE QUE NON.

NON?

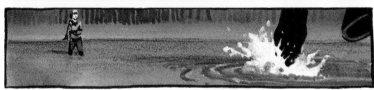

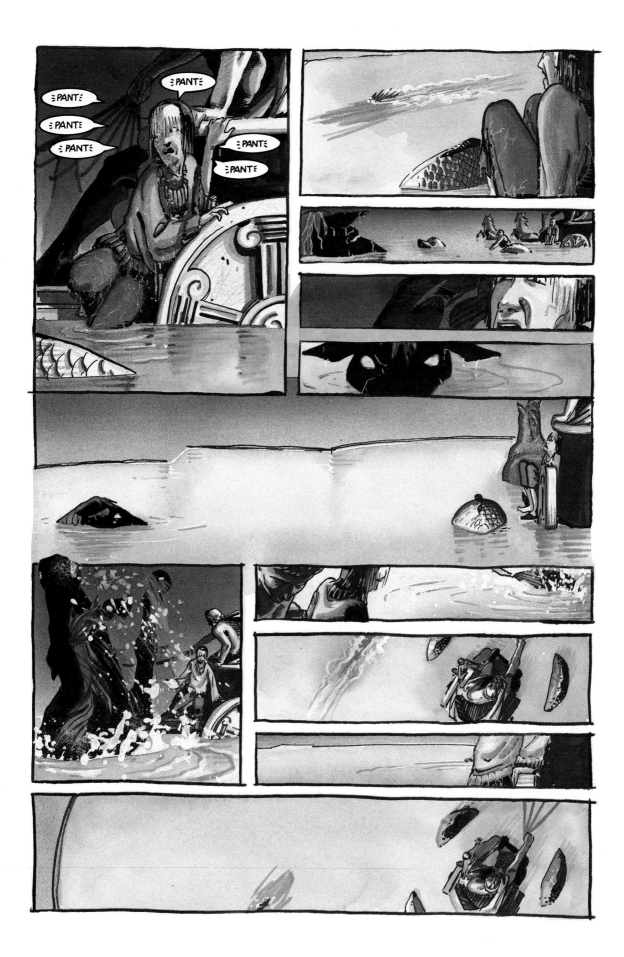

Fin